W9-CKI-676

BABY FLO
FLORENCE MILLS LIGHTS UP THE STAGE

by ALAN SCHROEDER

illustrated by

CORNELIUS VAN WRIGHT

and YING-HWA HU

LEE & LOW BOOKS INC. *New York*

To Joanne Ligamari, whose work touches so many lives—A.S.

To Gwendolyn—C.V.W. and Y.H.

This is a story about the childhood of the American entertainer Florence Mills (1896–1927). Reliable information about her early years is limited, and some details and dialogue have been imagined for storytelling purposes. In the interest of accuracy, it should be noted that Florence's vocal debut took place not in a butcher shop, as portrayed here, but in a less savory establishment. The stage name of "Mills," incidentally, was given to Florence when she was four years old. Her parents presumably did not think that a black woman could make it in show business with the last name of Winfrey.

Those who wish to learn more about Mills's life and exciting career should seek out Bill Egan's *Florence Mills: Harlem Jazz Queen* (Scarecrow Press, 2004).

—A.S.

Text copyright © 2012 by Alan Schroeder
Illustrations copyright © 2012 by Cornelius Van Wright and Ying-Hwa Hu

LEE & LOW BOOKS Inc., 95 Madison Avenue, New York, NY 10016
leeandlow.com

Manufactured in Singapore by Tien Wah Press, February 2012

Book design by Christy Hale
Book production by The Kids at Our House

The text is set in Arno Pro. The illustrations are rendered in watercolor.
10 9 8 7 6 5 4 3 2 1
First Edition

Library of Congress Cataloging-in-Publication Data

Schroeder, Alan.
Baby Flo : Florence Mills lights up the stage / by Alan Schroeder ;
illustrated by Cornelius Van Wright and Ying-Hwa Hu. — 1st ed.
p. cm.
Summary: "A biography of African American entertainer Florence Mills, an internationally renowned dancer, singer, and comedian of the Harlem Renaissance era, focusing on how she began her career as a child. Includes author's note and historical photographs"—Provided by publisher.
ISBN 978-1-60060-410-2 (hardcover : alk. paper)
1. Mills, Florence, 1896-1927—Juvenile literature. 2. African American singers—Biography—Juvenile literature. I. Van Wright, Cornelius. II. Hu, Ying-Hwa. III. Title.
ML420.M5132S37 2012
782.42165092—dc23
[B]
2011036553

STRAIGHT UP: Florence was a remarkable child, and that's a fact. She could sing before she was hardly out of diapers. And she won her first medal for dancing while other children were still learning their ABCs. Later, when Florence became famous and had her name up in lights, folks back in Washington, D.C. weren't the least bit surprised. They had known all along that someday Baby Flo would become a star. It was just a matter of time. . . .

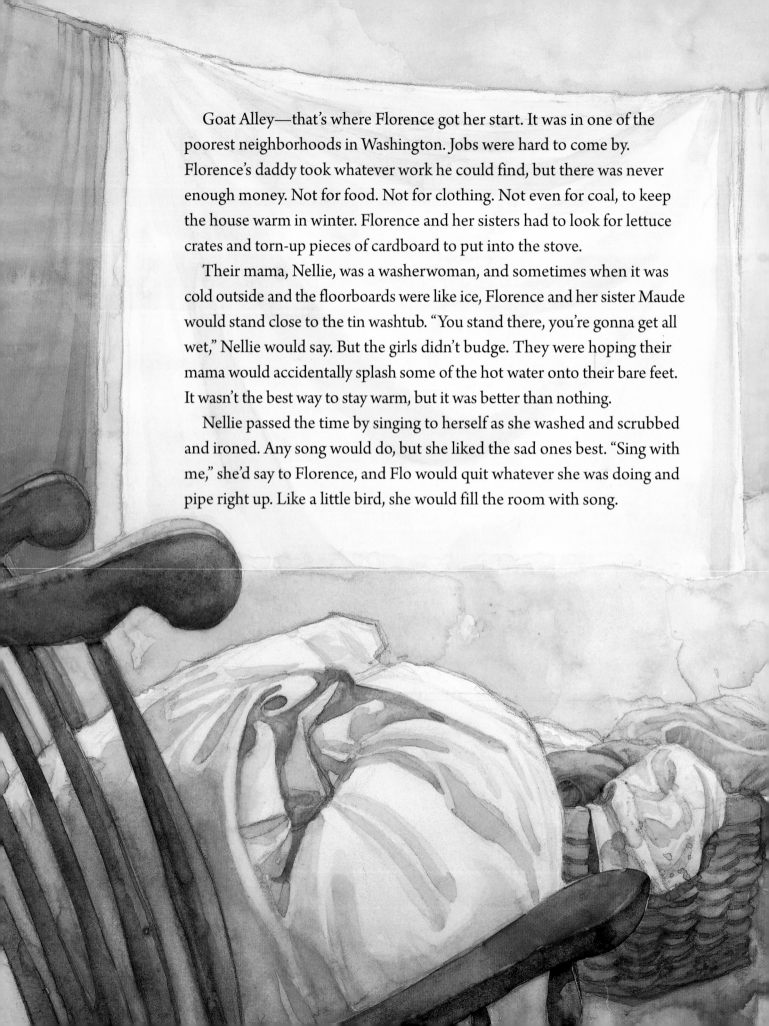

Goat Alley—that's where Florence got her start. It was in one of the poorest neighborhoods in Washington. Jobs were hard to come by. Florence's daddy took whatever work he could find, but there was never enough money. Not for food. Not for clothing. Not even for coal, to keep the house warm in winter. Florence and her sisters had to look for lettuce crates and torn-up pieces of cardboard to put into the stove.

Their mama, Nellie, was a washerwoman, and sometimes when it was cold outside and the floorboards were like ice, Florence and her sister Maude would stand close to the tin washtub. "You stand there, you're gonna get all wet," Nellie would say. But the girls didn't budge. They were hoping their mama would accidentally splash some of the hot water onto their bare feet. It wasn't the best way to stay warm, but it was better than nothing.

Nellie passed the time by singing to herself as she washed and scrubbed and ironed. Any song would do, but she liked the sad ones best. "Sing with me," she'd say to Florence, and Flo would quit whatever she was doing and pipe right up. Like a little bird, she would fill the room with song.

Every day at three o'clock Nellie would drop the clean laundry into a big white sack. Carefully, she'd balance the sack on top of her head. Then, taking Flo by the hand, she'd set out to make her deliveries.

Nellie had all sorts of customers. Rich white women. Families with kids. Store owners. Schoolteachers. She even did laundry for the butchers over on L Street, but only because they paid so well. She had to use lots of bleach and scrub hard before she could get the stains out of the butchers' aprons.

One afternoon, for fun, the butchers asked Florence if she would sing them a song. Any little tune she knew.

Problem was, Florence had never sung in public before.

"Go on," her mother said softly. "Just pretend you're at home singing with me."

So Florence did. With her eyes half closed, she sang two old Irish songs— real sad ones. "Mother Machree" and "Little Grey Home in the West." You should have seen those big men afterward! Half had tears streaming down their faces. The other half were too surprised to cry. *Where had a three-year-old learned to sing like that?* they wondered. The next thing Florence knew, the butchers were pressing money into her hand. Dimes, nickels, quarters, half-dollars. Then they begged her to sing the same two songs again.

Later, at home, Nellie counted the money. Then she counted it again. Three dollars and eighty-five cents! That was more than she made doing laundry.

She put the money in a safe place. Then she asked Florence how many songs she knew. "I know lots!" said Florence.

Nellie grinned. "Well, get ready, girl, 'cause you're gonna learn lots more!"

Florence worked hard and learned everything her mother taught her. At night, when her daddy came home feeling tired and discouraged, Florence would make him smile by singing and dancing for him.

"You're pretty good," John remarked. "You must have got that from my side of the family."

"In your dreams!" said Nellie. "She got it from me, that's who. Fool!"

After a couple of months, Nellie and John decided it was time to show off their little girl. John had a friend who was the manager of the Bijou Theatre in Washington. The manager heard Florence sing and said yes, he'd be delighted to put her in the show. And that's how Florence Mills began her career, at age three, wearing a nightgown on the stage of the Bijou, holding a candle, and singing a lullaby to the audience.

She got off to a good start, but halfway through, something happened. It was scary standing on that big stage all by herself, and suddenly Florence burst into tears. Her sister had to come out and lead her offstage. But the audience applauded anyway. There weren't many three-year-olds who could do what she'd done, let alone do it so well. Nope, not many at all.

One of the amazing things about Florence Mills was that she could dance as well as she could sing. Some said better. If she was playing outdoors and happened to hear music, her whole face would light up. "Uh-oh," her sister Maude would say. "Here she goes again."

Florence couldn't stop what came next even if she'd wanted to. With a big grin, she'd start clapping out the beat. Then off she'd go, dancing her way from one end of the block to the other. She danced so fast, it seemed to the other children that her feet hardly touched the pavement. Even the neighbor ladies would hang out the windows when Florence got going. It was always a treat, they said, to watch that child move.

At that time the most popular dance was the cakewalk, a high-stepping, high-strutting, look-at-me sort of dance that people couldn't get enough of. Florence picked it up real easy. She'd cakewalk her way to the market, to school—

Why, she'd even cakewalk her way into church on Sunday. "You just stop it now!" the minister would say. "I believe the devil's in your feet!"

Every month, it seemed, there were cakewalk contests in Washington. Florence entered as many as she could, and she usually won, too. That's how good she was. By the time she was six, she had a whole slew of medals hanging around her neck.

Word began to spread that there was an amazing little girl living in Goat Alley. Baby Flo was her name, and she could dance the pants off anybody. Well, the elegant men and women in Washington just had to see that. Fancy, horse-drawn carriages began to pull up in front of 23 Goat Alley. To the neighbors' astonishment, Florence would come prancing out, with her medals around her neck, like Cinderella going to the ball.

"You be good now," her mother would say, "and don't you be gone long!"

Then Florence would be driven off to some fancy house, where she would sing and dance for the powerful people of Washington. One of them, an ambassador's wife, gave her a shiny bracelet for teaching her guests how to do the cakewalk. Florence was mighty proud of that bracelet. For a long time she wouldn't take it off for anything. Not at bath time, not for bed. That bracelet was better than all her medals put together.

One wintry night Florence and her father were on the street, returning home, when they passed by the Bijou Theatre. John gave a little laugh. "I'll never forget that time you burst out crying in the middle of your song," he said.

Florence was embarrassed. "Please, Daddy, don't make fun of me," she begged.

John laughed again. "I ain't makin' fun o' you. I'm just rememberin', that's all." He gave Florence's shoulder a squeeze. "I was mighty proud of you that night—havin' the courage to get up there and sing like that. I know I couldn't a done it."

"I wish I hadn't cried," Florence said. "Tell me, Daddy, would you've cried?"

John grinned. "Of course not. I'd a *fainted*!" He pointed at the marquee hanging above. "Someday . . . ," he said, "someday we're gonna see your name up there in lights."

"Maybe," said Florence. But she sounded doubtful.

"No maybe about it," John said firmly. "It'll happen."

In 1903, when Florence was seven, a popular black show came to town. It was called *The Sons of Ham*, and Florence was thrilled to learn that one evening there was going to be a dancing contest during the intermission.

"Can I enter?" she asked.

"Of course," her mother said. "But it's not a cakewalk contest. It's a buck-and-wing contest, and that's somethin' altogether different."

"What's buck-and-wing?"

"Well . . . ," said Nellie. "It's a lot of tapping, for one thing. And a whole bunch more thrown in."

"Don't worry," John said. "I can teach you the steps."

The contest was only three days away. From a box under his bed, John retrieved his harmonica. Then, to the sound of his own lively music, he performed a buck dance in the middle of the room. He kept it simple, nothing fancy, so Florence could follow every step.

"Easy as pie," John said when he was finished. "Now it's your turn."

But the buck-and-wing was a harder dance to learn than the cakewalk. There were more turns, more steps to remember, and Florence kept forgetting which foot to come down on. "No, no," her papa kept saying. "It's right—right—shuffle left—*then* the ball change! Try it again. And not so fast this time."

Finally Thursday arrived—the night of the contest. Florence was so nervous she could hardly eat her supper. When she and her father arrived at the Empire Theatre, they discovered that seventeen people had signed up for the contest. That worried Florence. There had never been more than eight or nine at the cakewalk contests.

"When it's my turn to go on," she asked her daddy, "will you stand in the wings where I can see you?"

John shook his head. "You don't need to be lookin' off into the wings," he said. "Keep your eyes front and center."

"But where're you gonna be?" Florence asked. "I want to know."

"In my seat, that's where—applaudin' my fool head off!"

Florence had to wait until intermission for the contest to begin. Then she had to wait another half hour for her name to be called. The emcee grinned when he saw how little she was.

"Ladies and gents," he announced, "I got a real treat for you. Comin' up next is a pint-sized dynamo. I give you—the one, the only . . . 'Baby Florence' Mills!"

There was a drumroll. The clarinets began to wail, and the trumpets went *tat-a-tat-tat!* Bathed in a pretty blue light, Florence came dancing out from the wings. She started off slowly, tapping her way to the front of the stage.

Then, as the music picked up speed, she began to dance faster. "Hot feet!" she heard someone yell. "Tear it up, girl!" Pretty soon Florence was dancing as fast as she could.

When she was finished, the whole house rocked
with applause. But the buck-and-wing was a tricky dance.
Florence wished she'd had more practice.

The dancers all came out together to take a bow. Then the judge strutted onstage.

"What a night this has been!" he declared. "One sensational dancer after another. But I'm sure you'll agree that one little lady stood out. The winner is . . . Miss Clarice Johnson! Let's all give Clarice a big hand!"

The rest of the dancers were shooed off into the wings. "So," Florence said to herself, "I didn't win after all."

"Don't give it another thought," John said when he met her backstage. "I thought you did real good, 'specially the part where you kicked your leg up high. I'm tellin' you, Flo, you're a born entertainer."

Florence nodded. But secretly she felt disappointed. She had so wanted to win!

They were about to leave when the manager of the theater came running up.

"I'm glad I caught you." He sounded out of breath. "Listen," he said to Florence, "how would you like to be a part of the show—*The Sons of Ham*?"

Florence couldn't tell if the man was joking or not.

"But, mister," she said, "I didn't win. That Clarice lady did."

The manager scoffed. "What do I care about a medal? I saw what you did out there, and I heard the folks, and they was goin' crazy. Now, listen up," he said. "Every night for the next week I'm gonna have you perform at intermission. First you're gonna sing a song, somethin' peppy; then you'll dance, just like you did tonight. You do that, I'll give you twenty-five cents a night. Is it a deal?"

Florence looked up at her father. He gave her a warm nod.

"You betcha!" she told the manager.

Outside on the sidewalk, Florence couldn't stop spinning around, she was so excited. She couldn't wait to tell her mother the good news!

"I feel like celebrating," said John. "Let's go get some ice cream."

Just then a workman in overalls came out and set up a ladder in front of the theater. With a small bucket in his hand, he climbed up and began adding letters to the electric marquee. Florence and her father watched him. When he was done, the man began to climb back down the ladder.

Florence, wide-eyed, looked up at the sign. It read:

Comedy Hit! The Sons of Ham
Starring Charles Hart & Dan Avery
Special Added Attraction—One Week Only!
"Baby Florence" Mills

She couldn't believe it. Neither could John.

"There it is," he whispered. "I told you it would happen, didn't I? Your name, up in lights!"

The two of them stood for a long time looking up at the electric sign. Then, together, hand in hand, they headed down the street to Tucker's to get some ice cream.

STARRING CHARLES HART & DAN AV

SPECIAL ADDED ATTRACTION—ONE WEEK

"BABY FLORENCE" MILLS

AUTHOR'S NOTE

The song that Florence sang in *The Sons of Ham* was peppy, indeed—"Hannah from Savannah." The *Washington Star* wrote of her professional debut: "The peerless child artist who has appeared before the most exclusive set in Washington, delighting them with her songs and dances, is appearing this week at the Empire. . . . Baby Florence made a big hit and was encored for dancing."

Florence Mills in *Dixie to Broadway*, 1924

Because she started performing at such an early age, some may think that Florence was pushed into it, but that was not the case. She was happy, of course, to be able to help her family financially, but the main reason that she sang and danced was for pleasure. As one relative put it, "Florence loved to dance, to spread joy and happiness."

Over the next several years, Florence continued to work hard, honing her singing and dancing skills. Around 1909 she and her two older sisters formed a musical act and were soon performing in theaters up and down the Atlantic seaboard. Olivia and Maude, who were in their twenties, eventually quit the act, but Florence continued on, determined to make a name for herself in show business.

Like every performer on the black circuit, Florence had to put up with segregated railroad cars, run-down theaters, and managers who sometimes tried to cheat her out of her salary. But she remained cheerful and optimistic, rarely uttering a bad word about anyone. Her race, remarkably, does not appear to have hindered her career. In that respect, Florence was far luckier than most African American performers.

In 1917 she joined a popular vaudeville group, the Tennessee Ten. One member of that company was a

Florence in *Dover Street to Dixie* at the London Pavilion, 1923

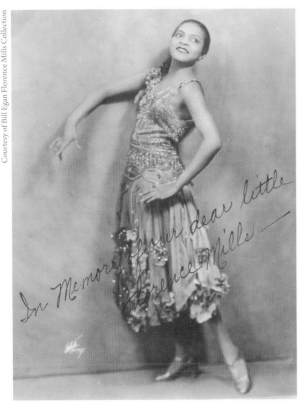

Florence in *Plantation Revue*, 1923

comic live wire named U. S. Thompson, who danced, cracked jokes, and conducted the orchestra. He and Florence fell in love and, after a long courtship, they were married in 1921.

Florence's big break came a few months later when she joined the cast of the hit musical *Shuffle Along*. Her performance was well received—so much so that, to her astonishment, she suddenly became the most popular black female entertainer in New York. Every aspect of her talent was praised: her beautiful, birdlike singing; her sensational dancing style; her pathos; her flair for comedy.

After *Shuffle Along*, Florence starred in a wildly successful cabaret show at the Plantation Room, a swanky nightclub atop the Winter Garden Theater in New York. Then, in 1923 she sailed to London to appear in the show *Dover Street to Dixie*. Her success in England was instantaneous. The word *genius* began to appear regularly in her reviews.

For the next few years, everything that Florence appeared in was successful: musical comedy, cabaret acts—even, on one occasion, a classical music recital in New York. Her fans included Charlie Chaplin, Duke Ellington, Paul Robeson, Bill "Bojangles" Robinson, and songwriter Irving Berlin, who considered her the "greatest of all colored performers."

Then tragedy intervened. Florence was at the height of her fame when she developed tuberculosis. An operation failed to save her life, and she died on November 1, 1927, at the age of just thirty-one. Her funeral, held a few days later, was a scene of near pandemonium. Five thousand people filled the A.M.E. Church to pay their last respects; thousands more stood outside, visibly and audibly distraught. The day after, describing the scene of the funeral,

Florence, mid-1920s

a reporter wrote, "Florence Mills played to her last 'house' yesterday. It was the greatest show Harlem ever has had, or is likely to have again."

Among those who were saddened by Florence's passing was composer and bandleader Duke Ellington. Not long after her funeral, he wrote a piece of music called "Black Beauty." It was one of his prettiest compositions, and many people believe that he had Florence in mind when he wrote it. In 1943, when "Black Beauty" was performed at Carnegie Hall, it was subtitled "Portrait of Florence Mills."

One of Florence's producers remarked that had it not been for the racial prejudice of the day, she would have been regarded as one of the half dozen greatest theatrical performers of the twentieth century. While that may be true, there are other reasons why Florence Mills is not well remembered. If film footage of her exists, it has not been discovered; the few recordings that she made have similarly vanished. The tremendous talent that Florence possessed lives on only in faded newspaper clippings and in the memories of those fortunate enough to have seen her.

Mourners crowding the streets of Harlem on the day of Florence Mills's funeral, November 6, 1927